A Dog for Everyone

Katrina Streza

xist Publishing

There is a dog for everyone
If only they will look,

To find a special best friend,
You'll want to read this book!

A bulldog always looks grumpy
Even when he is glad.
His wrinkles and short legs make him look old,
But he's younger than your dad!

Bulldog

Beagle

Beagles are known for their howl,
They're louder than a horn.
Their long ears will make you laugh
Even when you are forlorn.

If you'd like a guard dog,
A German Shepherd will be true.
Beware that they may bark a lot
But they will always protect you.

German Shepherd

Chihuahua

Chihuahuas are small with very large ears,
Some say that they look like a rat,
But their sweet personality makes them so fun
Unless they see a big cat.

Bernese Mountain Dogs have giant paws,
And a big tail that might knock you down.
But they're loving and gentle with long-flowing fur
Of a rich black and beautiful brown.

Bernese Mountain Dog

Labrador

A Labrador will adore water,
She'll splash you if you get too close.
She will be happy if you like to play fetch,
She will chase all the balls your dad throws.

Poodles are thought to be silly,
Because of the way they are groomed,
But they're bright hunting dogs who can learn many trick
Like dancing all over the room!

Poodle

Alaskan Malamute

An Alaskan Malamute is a snow dog
Don't let them get too hot!
They love their family but can run fast
So keep their leashes taut.

A Dachshund is known as a wiener dog
Because of their short and long stature.
They like to be pet behind their ears,
Their legs aren't long enough to scratch there.

Dachshund

Basset Hound

Basset Hounds look sad
Even on their happiest day.
It's because their face is so droopy,
But they still love to lick you and play.

A Greyhound is the fastest dog,
Some even run in a race.
But be careful or they might hurt their hip,
And then they'll have a sad face.

Greyhound

Samoyed

If you think you want a Samoyed,
Be ready to run with them for a while!
They can pull sleds and play funny games
And will always give you a smile.

Terriers can still be hunting dogs
To catch rabbits, foxes, or rats.
They are not afraid of anything
They MUST learn to not chase cats.

Terrier

Mastiff

Mastiffs are very large dogs
With big jaws and a smiling face.
They love to be hugged and petted,
And they love to stay in one place.

A Shih Tzu is a companion dog,
They are known for their long silky coat.
They need to be brushed every day
From their tail up to their throat.

Shih Tzu

A shelter dog can be the best dog
If you train them right from the start.
No matter their breed they can love you;
Expanding the size of your heart.

If you have the time and the energy
To love and take care of a dog,

I hope you will think very hard
Would you rather snuggle or jog?

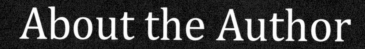
About the Author

Katrina Streza lives on a small ranch in Southern California with her family, twelve chickens, two cats, two dogs, one horse, one baby goat and one very noisy dove.

While receiving her Master's Degree in Education at Pepperdine University, Katrina decided that her goal was to make class so fun her students wouldn't realize they were learning. She's applied that philosophy while teaching and tutoring kids from kindergarten to college.

More books by Katrina

Text Copyright © Katrina Streza 2012
All images licensed from Fotolia
All Rights Reserved. No portion of this book may be reproduced
without express permission from the publisher.
First Edition
ISBN: 9781623953331 eISBN: 9781623953355
Published in the United States by Xist Publishing www.xistpublishing.com
PO Box 61593 Irvine, CA 92602

xist Publishing

66681076R10024

Made in the USA
Middletown, DE
14 March 2018